I am growing

First published in the U.S. in 1992 by Carolrhoda Books, Inc.

Copyright © 1991 Firefly Books Ltd., Hove, East Sussex.
First published 1991 Firefly Books Ltd.

Library of Congress Cataloging-in-Publication Data

Suhr, Mandy.
    I am growing / by Mandy Suhr; illustrated by Mike Gordon.
        p.   cm. – (I'm alive)
    Summary: Explains, in easy-to-read text, that we need food, sleep, and exercise to grow.
    ISBN 0-87614-734-1 (lib. bdg.)
    1. Growth–Juvenile literature. 2. Children–Growth–Juvenile literature. [1. Growth.] I. Gordon, Mike, ill. II. Title. III. Series: Suhr, Mandy. I'm alive.
QP84.S84 1992
612.6′5–dc20   91-34840
                                                                    CIP
                                                                    AC

Printed in Belgium by Casterman, S.A.
Bound in the United States of America

1 2 3 4 5 6 7 8 9 10 01 00 99 98 97 96 95 94 93 92

I am growing

written by Mandy Suhr

illustrated by Mike Gordon

I'm alive!

☘ Carolrhoda Books, Inc./Minneapolis

When I was born, I was only this
big. Everyone looked huge!
But as the weeks
went by…

5

I grew bigger.
I grew heavier.

I learned to crawl . . .

and then to walk.

I learned to talk . . .

dog!

and to paint.

I learned to write . . .

and to read.

And all this
happened because I was growing.

Growing is a funny thing. It seems to happen without your noticing.

But you are growing all the time.

My mom and dad say I need
lots of things to make me grow.

Milk helps make my teeth and
bones strong.

Fruits and vegetables
help make
me healthy.

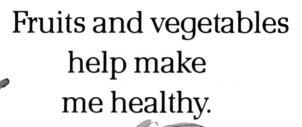

Bread and beans,
meat and fish,
eggs and cheese
help make my
muscles strong.

I need lots of exercise so that all
the parts of my body will grow
strong and healthy.

I also need to get plenty of
sleep, because growing can be
very tiring.

Plants grow too. I planted a tiny
seed just like this   and soon it
will grow into a plant.

Plants need
food from the soil . . .

sunshine...

and water...

to make
them grow.

Animals start out as little babies just as people do. My cat just had six kittens.

Soon they will grow big enough to go outside.

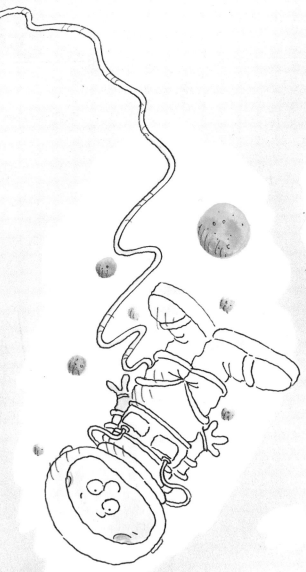

I wonder what
I will be when
I grow up?

Can you guess what these babies
will grow up to be?

23

A note to adults

I'm Alive is a series of books designed especially for preschoolers and beginning readers. These books look at how the human body works and develops. They compare the human body to plants and animals that are already familiar to children.

Here are some activities that use what kids already know to help them learn more about how plants, animals, and people grow.

Activities

1. Make a baby book. Collect photographs of yourself when you were younger. Talk to someone who knew you as a baby. Ask what you were like, and draw pictures. How have you changed since you were a baby?

2. Plant some seeds. Find a cup or a pot or even a milk carton and plant carrot, bean, or flower seeds. Put them in a window and wait for them to grow. Don't forget to water them when they get dry. Draw a picture of how they have changed after every two or three days.

3. Visit a wildlife park, farm, or zoo. See if you can spot some baby animals. Look at their parents. What are the differences between the adults and the babies?

4. How fast do you grow? Take off your shoes, stand next to a door or wall, and have someone mark your height with tape. Measure yourself again in a couple of months. Did you grow?